SHORT TALES

NORSE MYTHS

TYR

Adapted by
Christopher E. Long

Illustrated by
Mike Dubisch

visit us at www.abdopublishing.com

Published by Magic Wagon, a division of the ABDO Publishing Group, 8000 West 78th Street, Edina, Minnesota, 55439. Copyright © 2011 by Abdo Consulting Group, Inc. International copyrights reserved in all countries. All rights reserved. No part of this book may be reproduced in any form without written permission from the publisher.

Short Tales ™ is a trademark and logo of Magic Wagon.

Printed in the United States of America, North Mankato, Minnesota.
032010
092010
This book contains at least 10% recycled materials.

Adapted Text by Christopher E. Long
Illustrations by Mike Dubisch
Colors by Wes Hartman
Edited by Stephanie Hedlund and Rochelle Baltzer
Interior Layout by Kristen Fitzner Denton
Book Design and Packaging by Shannon Eric Denton

Library of Congress Cataloging-in-Publication Data

Long, Christopher E.
  Tyr / adapted by Christopher E. Long ; illustrated by Mike Dubisch.
    p. cm. -- (Short tales. Norse myths)
  ISBN 978-1-60270-570-8
  1. Tyr (Norse deity)--Juvenile literature. I. Dubisch, Michael. II. Title.
  BL870.T97L66 2009
  398.209363'01--dc22
                                        2008032499

THE NORSE GODS

ODIN:
The All-Father
of the Gods

FRIGGA:
Queen of
the Gods

BALDUR:
The Best Loved
of the Gods

FORSETI:
God of
Justice

HEIMDALL:
The Guardian
of Asgard

HOD:
God of Winter

THOR:
God of Thunder

TYR:
God of War

HERMOD:
Messenger of
the Gods

FREYR:
God of Weather

LOKI:
The Trickster

FREYA:
Goddess of
Beauty and Love

Mythical Beginnings

Tyr was the bravest and boldest of the Norse gods. As the god of battle and justice, he was known to keep his word at all costs. He was Odin's right-hand man.

Tyr was a powerful, skilled warrior. He went into battle with a clear head. He fought only for justice and honor.

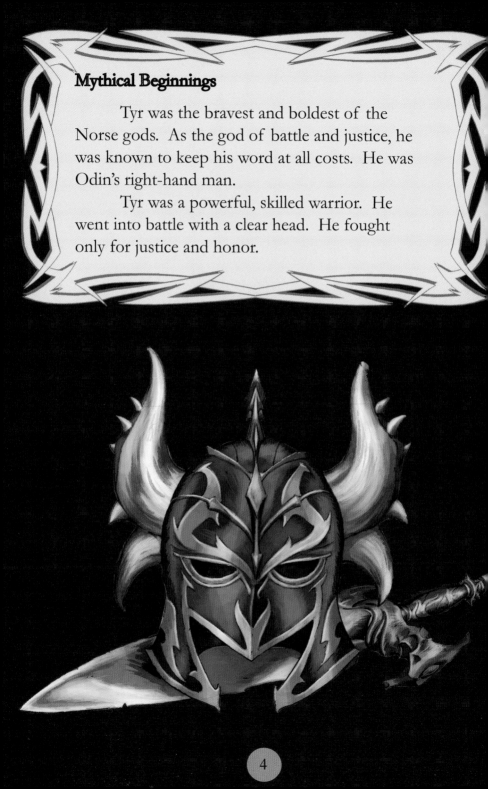

Before humankind walked the earth, Norse gods ruled the heavens. Of all these gods, the bravest and boldest was Tyr. Tyr was the god of battle and justice.

The history of Tyr was lost. Some said Odin was his father. Some said Tyr was the first god to emerge out of the darkness into the light.

All agree that Tyr was an honorable god. He lived his life based on a warrior's code of conduct. He was a skilled fighter, but he only fought in just wars.

Around this time, a giant named Loki and his wife, Angrboda, had a son. Their son, Fenrir, was a fierce wolf monster.

The gods soon learned of a prophecy. It said Fenrir would destroy Odin.

"We must prevent this from happening," Tyr said.

"Tyr, how do you propose to stop Fenrir?" Odin asked.

"He is too strong and powerful," Frigga said.

"He might be strong and powerful, but Fenrir is not smart," Tyr said, smiling. "We will trick the beast."

The gods put their plan to trick Fenrir in motion. Tyr struggled to break a chain fastened around a boulder.

"Let me try, Tyr!" Thor shouted. "I can surely break that chain."

Fenrir approached the gods as they played their game with the chain.

"What are you doing?" Fenrir snarled.

"We're seeing who's strong enough to break this chain," Tyr replied.

"I am strong enough to break that chain," Fenrir growled.

"Then come here and let me tie it around you," Tyr said.

"Will you let me out if I can't break the chain?" Fenrir asked.

"Of course we will," Thor laughed.

Fenrir slowly approached Tyr.

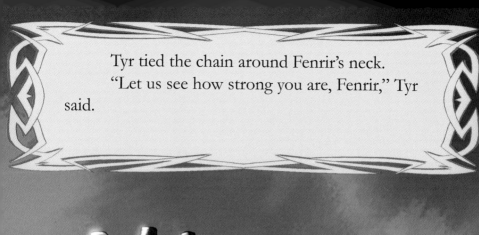

Tyr tied the chain around Fenrir's neck.
"Let us see how strong you are, Fenrir," Tyr
said.

Fenrir dug his paws into the ground and pulled against the chain. He growled as he strained to break it. Tyr watched as Fenrir lunged forward. Soon, Fenrir snapped the chain with a loud crack.

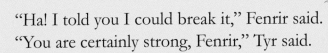

"Ha! I told you I could break it," Fenrir said.

"You are certainly strong, Fenrir," Tyr said.

"I like this game," Fenrir said. "I'll come back tomorrow to play again."

Tyr went into the Forgotten Cave, the home of the dwarves. He asked the dwarves to weave an enchanted rope.

Tyr wanted the rope to be strong enough to bind Fenrir forever. The dwarves worked through the night to make the special rope. As they worked, they chanted spells to make the rope unbreakable.

The next day, Fenrir waited for Tyr.

"I didn't think you were going to show, Tyr," Fenrir said.

"Let's see if you're strong enough to break this rope," Tyr replied.

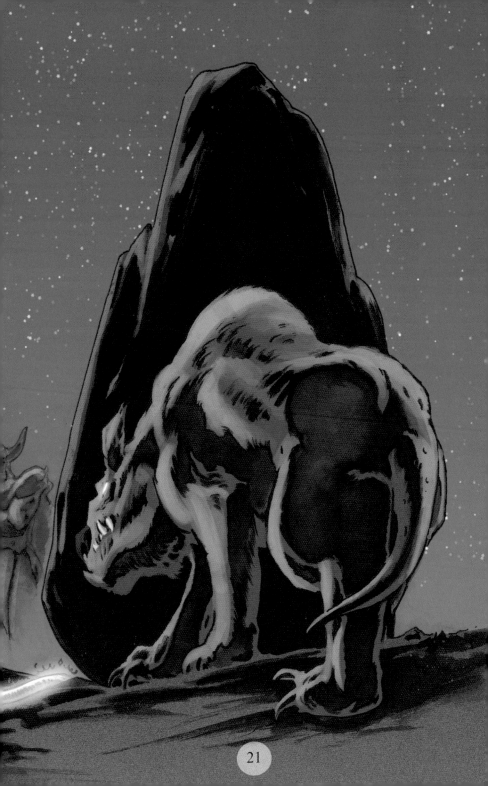

"If I can't break that magic rope, you'll leave me bound," Fenrir said as he backed away from the rope.

"That won't be a problem if you're strong enough to break it," Tyr said.

"I want a sign of good faith before I play your game," Fenrir said.

"What do you require?" Tyr asked.

"Put your right hand in my mouth," Fenrir snarled.

"If I can't break the rope, and you don't release me," Fenrir said, "I'll bite off your hand." Tyr agreed, and placed his right hand in Fenrir's mouth.

Fenrir struggled to break the magic rope, but he couldn't. It was too strong.

"I can't break this rope," Fenrir said. "Release me."

"I'm afraid I can't do that," Tyr answered.

"But I will bite off your hand, Tyr," Fenrir growled.

Tyr stared at Fenrir for a moment, before saying, "Yes, I know."

"A deal is a deal," Tyr grimaced. "And I will honor it."

"You are a fool!" Fenrir snarled. Then he bit off Tyr's hand.

"Better an honorable fool than just a fool," Tyr responded.

"Release me! Release me!" Fenrir shouted as Tyr walked away. But the gods ignored him. They left him bound by the magic rope.

Many years later, Fenrir broke free of the magic rope. He joined his father's army as they battled with the gods.

The battle was called Ragnarok. Tyr fought bravely that day.

As the flames of Ragnarok died out, a beautiful new world was born. The old gods were gone forever. But the Norse people would always remember the heroic Tyr. They honored him by naming Tuesday after him!